HAWKE FAMILY CHRISTMAS

GWYN MCNAMEE

THE HAWKE FAMILY

Antonia and Sam "The Savage" Hawke

SAVAGE COLLISION

Savage Hawke & Danika Eriksson
|
Kennedy Hawke

STONE COLD

Stone Hawke & Nora Eriksson
/ \
Isaac Hawke   Coen Hawke

TAINTED SAINT

Solomon "Saint" Clarke & Caroline Brooks
/ \
Pope Clarke   Bishop Clarke

TORTURED SKYE

Skye Hawke & Gabe Anderson
/ \
Atlas Anderson   Astrid Anderson

BUILDING STORM

Storm Hawke (Matthews) & Landon McCabe
/ \
Angelina Matthews   Alessandra McCabe

STEELE RESOLVE

Luca "Steele" Abello & Byron Harris
|
Jude Harris-Abello (ad)

CHAPTER 1

SAVAGE

*T*he bathroom door opens, and Dani flips off the light before she steps out into the bedroom, still towel-drying her hair after her shower. Her eyes find me on the bed, and she freezes, stumbling a half-step.

A slow smile spreads across her pink lips. "Is that a Santa hat on your ass?"

I can't fight my grin, and I peer behind me at it before turning my attention back to my stunningly beautiful wife wrapped in a fluffy white robe. "Yep."

She giggles lightly as she approaches the bed. "Is there a reason for it?"

Raising a brow at her, I shrug slightly, propping

my face in my hand. "Because it's Christmas Eve..." I glance at the clock on the nightstand. "Actually, it's very early Christmas morning, and I thought it would be fun to do something festive. Had I set it over my hard cock instead, that would have been a bit vulgar, no?"

Dani laughs, the bright, airy sound filling the room and my heart with so much light and happiness that it makes my cock ache where it's pinned against the bed. She climbs up, letting her towel slip to the floor. "You? Vulgar? *Never.*" Another soft giggle slips from her mouth. "The man who told me on our first date that he couldn't stop thinking about how much he wanted to bury his face between my legs and his tongue in my pussy..."

"It was true. Still is." Grinning, I drag her toward me to press my lips to hers. Even after over seventeen years with this woman, I can never get enough of her —her smile, her laugh, her taste, her touch, her love.

I'd be fucking lost without her.

She melts into me, urging me onto my back with the Santa hat now stuck between the mattress and me, sprawled naked the wrong way across the bed. Dani doesn't seem to care. She throws one long bare leg over me, straddling my waist and pressing my hard cock against her hot core.

One shoulder of her robe slips down her arm, exposing her elegant collarbone, and I reach for the belt at her waist and tug the tie free, letting the soft terrycloth fall open completely.

Still slightly pink from her hot shower, her skin practically glows in the light from the lamp on the nightstand. I reach out and glide my fingers down her neck, over her collarbone, and down to her breast, twisting her nipple sharply.

"Fuck!" She jerks against me, her warm blue eyes heating with the same lust I always see there when I touch her. Shifting slightly, she grinds down on me, slipping up and down so the head of my cock slides against her clit. "What got into you tonight? I figured after midnight Mass, you'd want to go to sleep since we'll have to deal with the entire family tomorrow... errr, today."

I grin at her and tweak her other nipple, earning another sharp gasp. "With Kennedy at Storm and Landon's with the rest of the kids, it means we have the place to ourselves. That so rarely happens. I don't want to waste it. And while I was sitting out here, waiting for you to finish your shower, I couldn't stop picturing you naked in there, the hot water sluicing all over your beautiful curves. You know, once that sort of fantasizing starts, there's only one way to stop it—your cunt or mouth on my cock."

Her lips twitch, and she leans down and brushes them gently over mine, rolling her hips to glide her slick arousal all down my length. I groan into her mouth, wrapping my arms around her to tug her down fully against me. The press of her body against mine makes my cock twitch where it's pinned against her slick cunt.

I take her face in my palms and devour her mouth, angling her head to give me better access. She moans and adjusts her position to allow just the head of my dick to slip inside her.

"Fuck..." I mutter against her lips, tightening my grip on her face. "You have no idea what you do to me, woman."

She grins, humor flashing in her heated gaze. "Oh, I think I do, Mr. Hawke..."

With a slight adjustment of her hips, she sinks down fully onto me, taking me all the way to the hilt.

Sweet mother of God...

It feels sacrilegious to be thinking that and doing this on the day Mary gave birth—and only an hour after we got home from attending Mass with *almost* the whole Hawke clan—but when I think of religious experiences, being fucked by Danika is at the top of the list. So, I let go of any lingering guilt and concentrate on what I can feel, like her scalding heat encasing my cock.

She squeezes around me, lowering her mouth to mine again. "Were you thinking about this while we were sitting in church?"

Fuck.

This woman knows me too well...

"Maybe."

Dani grins and lifts her hips to slowly sink back down onto me, then grinds against my pelvis, rubbing her clit against it the way she likes. "I bet you were." She feathers her lips over mine, then shifts over to my ear as she rides me. "I bet you were thinking about the fact that we were going to have an empty house for the night, and I bet your cock was hard before I ever stepped into that shower..."

She's got me there.

Sitting in church, surrounded by the family, singing the hymns on one of the holiest days of the year, my mind kept drifting back to my stunningly beautiful and talented wife. Close to two decades later, she still occupies my thoughts and dreams the same way she did when she first stormed into my office, filled with rage and judgment, and called me a pussy peddler all those years ago.

Dani owns me—body, mind, and soul. She always will.

And she knows it.

The smug grin pulls at her lips as she slowly breaks down my control, rolling her hips and gliding up and down my cock agonizingly slowly. Each retreat feels like losing part of myself, but then she's right back, sinking down, taking me deep inside her and clenching around my flesh like she can't get close enough to me or take me far enough.

She presses her palms flat against my chest and leans back, allowing me to watch my glistening cock slip in and out of her. I grip her hips, helping guide her up and down, digging my fingers into the flesh I know will show the bruises tomorrow.

Seeing those marks on her only makes me crazier for her, and she is more than aware of it. Dani relishes her power over me, the way I melt for her and will do anything, give her anything she could ever want or need.

Even after all this time, I worry I won't be enough for her, that one day, she's going to come to her senses and leave my ass for someone who can be more for her, but in moments like this, I'm drawn back to that night she told me she loved me, when I was too broken to respond in kind.

She loved me then, when I was shattered and lost in my head, battling my demons, and she loves me now. I still see it in her eyes every time she looks at me.

Like now.

The warm blue I love swimming in locks on me, and she digs her nails into my pecs, the sharp bite of pain making my cock twitch inside her. She clamps around me tightly, then increases her pace, done with the languid ride and ready to race toward her release.

I'm right there with her.

My whole body heats, my skin hypersensitive to her touch, to the feel of the comforter under me, her pelvis pressed to mine...

Each grind down on me makes my balls tighten more. "Fuck, Dani..." I let my eyes drift closed, but when that tiny whimper slips from her lips, I open them, knowing she's about to come. "Come for me, baby."

She pulls her bottom lip between her teeth, her eyes squeezed closed. Hips grinding. Breasts swaying. Chest heaving. She's right there. So close.

This woman has *always* taken what she wants and needs, and watching her find her release has become the thing I crave more than anything in this world.

Her orgasm hits her, her mouth falling open on a gasp, and her hips falter for a moment before she finds her rhythm again to draw out mine. Seeing Danika come, the pure ecstasy overtaking her face, finally makes me unleash what I've been holding back.

I come deep inside her as she twitches and comes down from her own release. She collapses on top of me, burying her face against my neck, her damp blond locks falling all around us. I brush them away and drag my fingers down her spine. Dani shivers, snuggling herself even closer.

Wrapping my arms around her, I nuzzle my face against her hair. "You cold?"

"No." She shakes her head but shivers again. "Okay, maybe."

I chuckle and pull her face back. "It's cold in here; let's get under the covers."

She nods her agreement and rolls off me, my wet cock slipping free from inside her. "I need another shower."

Laughing, I roll over toward the head of the bed as she pulls the comforter and sheet back. "Probably..." I hold out a hand to her, and she slips hers into mine, allowing me to tug her down against me and drag the covers over us. "But I love knowing you're sleeping next to me with my cum still inside you."

Her lips twist into a scowl. "You have a filthy mind, Savage Hawke."

I grin at her. "I do, but that's what you love about me."

DANIKA

I love so many things about him.

His patience. How gentle and caring he is with me and Kennedy. What an incredible husband and father he's been. How determined he is to fight for the family, for all of his siblings and nieces and nephews, to ensure that we'll all have the type of future he never thought he could give us. His undaunting strength in the face of all the adversity he has confronted and all the losses he has suffered.

And I love the way he loves me unconditionally—even when I fuck up, even when I piss him off, even when he glowers at me, I can feel that heat radiating from his Caribbean-blue eyes that lets me know he's one second away from erupting.

In the end, I always know there's love there. Strong, welcoming arms and a safe place to land. Unconditional support from the man who stole my heart the moment he called me out for thinking he was a total scumbag.

It's what keeps me going every day and allows me to rest peacefully at night—Savage always beside me.

I nuzzle closer against him, pressing my cheek over his heart, listening to the steady beat, the same sound that has lulled me to sleep for so many years. "I think this is going to be a great Christmas."

He chuckles softly. His body shakes under me, and he wraps his arm around me to squeeze me tightly. "What makes you say that?"

I shrug. "I don't know. Something just feels different, like things are changing. Maybe because Kennedy isn't here tonight, and she's doing the sleepover with the kids at Storm's." I push up on my elbow and look at him, the slight graying at his temples and in his beard, the only real changes in him since the day I stormed into his office and told him off. "It's our first Christmas Eve without her here. The first morning we'll go to the fireplace and not have gifts from Santa there and in the stockings since we're opening everything at your mom's."

Savage's brow furrows. "Isn't that kind of sad, though? I don't know why it would make you feel like this is a 'great' thing."

Well, when he puts it like that...

"Sort of." I picture Kennedy as she was on her first Christmas, her blond curls and the excitement of tearing open presents. "I guess she isn't a baby anymore."

He barks out a laugh, his face lighting up. "She's sixteen, Dani. She hasn't been a baby for a *long* time. And sixteen-year-olds don't believe in Santa or need the fanfare of his arrival. She hasn't since she was what, seven or eight?"

I trail my finger across his chest. "I know. Thanks for reminding me how much I hate that she's growing up and throwing ice water on my good mood."

Savage tilts my chin up with a finger under it. "You don't hate that she's growing up. Neither of us particularly enjoyed diaper duty or midnight feedings. What you hate is that she's almost an adult and you can't control her anymore."

I scowl at him. "When could we *ever* control Kennedy?"

He grins and runs his fingers through my still-damp hair. "True. Since the moment she came into this world, it was clear she is so much like *you*."

The tiniest pang of annoyance hits my chest. "You say that like it's a bad thing."

Savage shakes his head. "Definitely not. While I hope she has more common sense than you and doesn't rush off chasing things the way you do stories without thinking about the consequences, I wouldn't want her to be like me." He inhales deeply. "I'm too…"

"You're too what?"

He glances up at the ceiling like he's trying to think of the right word. "Mercurial."

I laugh and press a kiss to the center of his chest. "You are definitely that, but you're also the strongest man I know."

"I don't know about that."

He's so bad at taking compliments. Even after all these years, he can't just accept how much I see in him.

"I do." I push up to press a chaste kiss to his lips. "You have proven it to me over and over again. Things may be changing, but I have a feeling it's for the better."

He raises a dark brow at me. "I guess we'll have to see." His gaze cuts to the clock. "We have to be at

Mom's in seven hours, and we still have to load all the presents into the car in the morning before we go."

"Okay, so what are you saying?" I grin at him. "That we should actually get some sleep?"

Throwing my leg across his pelvis, I slide my body fully over him, settling my core over his dick.

He groans. "Dani..."

"I have another idea."

Because he's right—we so *rarely* get time alone in the house, when we don't have to worry about whether Kennedy might come barging into our room unannounced.

We need to make good use of it while we have it...

I kiss my way down his chest, over his stomach, and toward his cock that's already hard again between us. He watches me with hooded eyes, his breaths coming short and sharp in anticipation. I slip my mouth around him, and the taste of both our releases dances across my tongue.

"Fucking hell, woman." He buries his fingers in my hair and tightens his grip as I suck him down, all the way to the back of my throat. "Fuck, your mouth is nuclear."

I laugh around his flesh, the vibration making his body twitch, then slowly withdraw, only to swallow him back. He grunts, and I wrap my hand around the base of his length and stroke as I work him over, building him quickly, doing it exactly the way I know he likes it.

He issues a low groan to let me know he's close, and his body tenses. I flick my tongue along that spot at the bottom of the head, and he erupts, shooting deep down my throat.

The moan that fills the room makes my clit ache, desperate to have him inside me again so quickly. I swallow every last drop and slowly lick him as he twitches one more time.

He opens his eyes and looks down at me as I grin. "Don't look so smug. You know I can do much worse to you."

I laugh as I settle over him. "I know. Are you offering?"

His eyes darken, but the phone on the nightstand rings, jerking both our heads in that direction.

He scowls. "It's almost two in the morning. Who the fuck would be calling now?"

I tense. "It can't be good news this time of night, right?"

He shakes his head, then reaches over and grabs his phone, glancing at the screen. "It's Luca; I need to take this."

"Of course."

Luca and Byron missing Mass was a little odd. It isn't like Luca not to be there, but he said he had something important to take care of and that he would be at Antonia's for Christmas Day. Still, he isn't the kind of man who calls at two in the morning to say a quick hello.

Savage slides his finger across the phone and brings it to his ear. "Hey, is everything all right?" He listens, his eyes darting to meet mine. "What do you mean, you *found* him?"

I raise a brow, and Savage presses his lips together in a firm line. His hand tightens around the phone, his knuckles whitening. Anger builds in his darkening eyes, and his shoulders tense.

"So, he's with Nora now?"

"*Nora?*" I mouth to him, and he shakes his head, indicating he'll fill me in once he's done with the call.

"No, that's fine. Bring him with you tomorrow, if you think he's up for it. I'll let Mom know in the morning to set one more place at the table. Okay. All right, I'll see you later."

Savage ends the call and tosses the phone onto the nightstand, scrubbing his hands over his face.

Dread coils around my spine. "What is it?"

He drops his hands, and his normally Caribbean-blue eyes, now darkened with concern and rage, meet mine almost reluctantly. "Byron and Luca found a little boy behind the club today."

"What?"

"Apparently, he was"—Savage sucks in a shaky breath—"trying to make some money..."

"Oh, God." My stomach turns, and I roll off him to the side to stare up at the ceiling. "Where are his parents?"

"Luca said something about the mom being dead. He's looking for the dad. They brought Nora over to examine the boy, Jude."

I glance over at him. "And they're going to bring him to your mom's house tomorrow?"

He shrugs. "It sounds like it."

"Jesus…what are they going to do with him? They can't…*keep* him?"

Savage gives me a hard smile. "I don't know. Stone is there, and he's trying to get some sort of emergency court order and approval from the Human Services Department so Jude can stay with them temporarily."

"Wow…"

There isn't anything else to say about it.

Suddenly, that warm, fuzzy feeling I had about what a great Christmas this would be disappears on a wave of worry and uncertainty.

CHAPTER 2

NORA

*S*tone sidles up behind me, pressing his hard body against my back, and drops his lips to my ear. "You need to stop staring at the door, angel."

I turn my head to look up at him, and his hard blue eyes meet mine, filled with the same concern I feel. "I wasn't."

He presses a quick kiss on my cheek. "You've been watching the door like you're a guard at Fort Knox since we got here." He motions with his hand holding his tonic and lime toward Nana's tree, where all the kids sit, opening their gifts. "You should be having a good time. Not worrying about when Luca and Byron are going to get here."

As if it's that easy...

The Christmas music fills the room, mixing with the laughter and chatter of everyone crammed in around the tree, and I turn my attention to Coen and Isaac tearing into their gifts excitedly. All that careful wrapping and bows, tossed aside in seconds once they see what's inside.

Isaac glances up at me, looking so much like his father—more and more every year that passes. He holds up his new gaming system. "Thanks, Mom. Thanks, Dad."

I smile at him, trying to push away my worry for another little boy who should be arriving soon. "You're welcome."

Coen scowls, staring at his gift—the science kit I swear he told us he wanted months ago. "Why did he get *that*, and I didn't?"

Stone releases a heavy sigh. "Because you're four years younger than him. Maybe when you're fifteen, we'll get one for you, too."

Coen pouts, but I try not to take it personally. He's at that weird age where everything upsets him, no matter *what* we say or do. There is no "right" with him now. I *pray* he makes it through it as fast as Isaac did and that when he turns thirteen soon, it doesn't get worse and he starts acting like my sweet, helpful boy again.

The rest of the kids excitedly thank their parents

and tear into other gifts, and my gaze cuts to the door again.

Stone's free hand comes up to rub at my arm. "You're really worried about Jude, aren't you?"

I sigh and finally turn to face him, quickly peeking around us to make sure no one's listening. Even though Savage, Stone, Dani, and I have already filled in everyone on what happened to Luca and Byron yesterday, we don't want any of the kids to overhear.

"I am." I shake my head, pressing my palms against his hard chest. "You don't understand how destroyed that boy was."

While Stone came to Luca and Byron's with me to meet Jude, he never entered the room when I did the exam. He never saw what had been done to that poor boy or how traumatized he is from the life his father has been forcing on him.

Stone's jaw hardens, and a muscle there tics as he tries to contain his anger. "I think I have some idea."

Of course, Luca and Byron filled him in while I examined Jude, and he's already made the calls to set things in motion for them to get temporary custody while things get sorted out. They should be meeting with Stone's contact at HSD this morning before they come here—something that *never* would have happened on Christmas Day without Stone pulling strings and calling in favors.

I sigh and drop my forehead to his chest. "I just

don't know how he's going to react to all this." I motion around me. "We're a lot, and that kid is traumatized more than anyone I've ever had come into the hospital."

That vacant look in his eyes mixed with the absolute terror—it isn't anything I can ever forget.

"I have them running every test I can think of on his blood just to make sure he's not sick with something we can't see, because who knows what the hell he was exposed to when…"

I can't even say the words, and Stone grasps my chin and tilts it up until I look at him.

"Your heart is too big, angel. You know that?"

I offer him a sad smile. "Yours is, too. You just don't like to admit it."

Stone grins at me. "Well, I don't want you spending the whole day worried and distracted. The kids will pick up on it."

"I know."

He lowers his head until his lips brush my ear again. "I have an idea, something that might take your mind off it."

I pull back slightly and narrow my eyes at him because I *know* that look and the promise in those words. "We are *not* having a quickie in your childhood bedroom again, Stone. Your mother almost caught us last time."

A slow grin tugs at his lips. "That would've made for a very interesting Thanksgiving, though, wouldn't it?"

My body heats at the memory of the way he made me come before our last holiday dinner even as I smack his arm.

He chuckles and leans in again. "I was worried you were going to spend the whole day dwelling on this, so I brought something for you."

I raise a brow at him. "Oh, yeah, what's that?"

Stone gives me that lecherous grin I always know means trouble, and I hiss at him.

"It better not be a coil of rope. You are not tying me up at your mother's house."

He releases a laugh that draws everyone's attention, and Storm and Landon both offer us knowing grins, while Caroline raises her mimosa toward us and Saint smiles. Gabe and Skye roll their eyes, but Savage and Dani return their focus to the kids and Nana, who's sitting in her high-back chair, watching all of them before she has to start on dinner.

Stone wraps his arm around my waist and tugs me fully against him. "Not a coil of rope. We'll save that for tonight when we get home." He kisses my cheek. "Maybe I'll even string you up on the hook since we got interrupted last night."

A shudder rolls through me. "Promises. Promises."

He tightens his grip on me. "I brought your favorite toy. You could go back to the bathroom, take off your panties, and slip these ones on right now."

I push back from him and glower. "You mean *your* favorite toy?"

Torture device is a more accurate description.

I could *never* forget how he used the vibrating panties on me while sitting in this very house at his mother's table when we first got together, and the reminder sends heat between my legs despite the complete inappropriateness of the situation.

Stone grins. "Semantics."

He brings his drink to his lips and takes a sip. I'm sure he'd much rather be enjoying a bourbon or mimosa with everyone else, but his continued sobriety over the last fifteen years has been the only thing that ever allowed this to work—and he's worked *hard* for it.

I know there were a lot of times he wanted to break, wanted to go down that road when the stresses of managing all the legal problems of Hawke Enterprises and having two young sons got to him and he would have loved to drown his problems in booze or cocaine. But we worked through those times together and used *other* outlets for his frustration and need for the illusion of control.

We did it together, just like we always will. Just

like he's trying to do now—using a naughty promise to try to distract me from my worry. And after so many years, the fact that he still looks at me with that fire in his eyes and still follows through on his threats makes goosebumps break out over my skin.

I feather my lips over his. "As much as I know you would enjoy toying with me today and distracting me, I think I need to keep an eye on the kids and the door. I don't know how Jude's going to react to any of this. He might need me."

Stone's gaze immediately softens, and he presses a kiss to my forehead. "You're such an incredible woman. You know that, right?"

"You've told me once or twice."

"But you don't always have to take care of everyone else." His gaze holds so much concern. "Sometimes, you have to take care of yourself, or let me do it."

I press my hand to his cheek. "You always do."

He tilts his head to brush his lips over my palm, then Isaac rushes over holding up his new gaming system.

"Can we set this up when we get home?"

Stone nods. "Sure, buddy." But he glances at Coen. "You know you're going to have to let your brother play it, too, right?"

Isaac scowls. "Why? He has his own gifts."

I turn to our oldest—and most stubborn—the one who's so much like his dad, who always wants to be in control of everything. "Because he's your brother, and you have to share, whether you like it or not."

The little smartass who has developed so much attitude in his teens raises his dark brows. "Did Aunt Dani always share with you as a kid?"

I laugh and look over at her, where she sits on Savage's lap, arm wrapped around his neck, as they watch Kennedy dig through her new makeup kit. "Your Aunt Danika was always a little selfish, and that's one reason I want to make sure you're not."

He scowls at me again but huffs and walks back to plop down onto the floor near the tree and next to Coen. Coen fiddles with one of his other gifts—a new Lego set—looking sullen. Isaac shows him the game system box and points to one of the games, and Coen's eyes light up.

Stone tugs me to his side, wrapping his arm around my shoulders as he takes another sip of his drink. "You're a good mom."

I look up at him. "You're a good dad."

He grins. "That's a lie, but thanks for saying so."

"You didn't have one, babe. All you had was—" I bite off the name instead of saying it, but it's too late, and a dark cloud settles over his eyes. "You didn't have the best male role model, but you've been incredible with them, practically raising them yourself while I was going to medical school and through my residency and fellowship. Don't underestimate how incredible you are—at being a dad and so many other things."

STONE

It's hard not to—knowing what I put Nora through, what I hid from her for so long and what the truth did to her, Dani, and their mother, what it and my choices did to *everyone*. She had every reason to push me away and never look back, to try to keep me from Isaac when he was born and cut me out of their lives. Yet, somehow, this magnificent woman has stuck by me and given me *life*.

I've done everything in my power since the day I came back to make it up to her, to atone for my sins and become a man she can be proud of, a good father to Isaac and Coen and husband to her, but sometimes, it still feels like I'm failing.

And seeing that boy last night, hearing Luca and Byron tell me how they found him and what had been happening outside one of *our* clubs, makes anger flare red hot like I haven't felt in years. Instantly, my mind placed Isaac and Coen in his shoes, and that need to protect Jude when I didn't even know him roared to the forefront.

None of us will ever let any harm come to him again, but we all know he has a long, bumpy road ahead that I fear we are wholly unprepared to help him navigate.

Nora's soft hand finds my cheek. "Where'd you go just now?"

I force a smile at her. "Nowhere, angel."

At least, nowhere good.

But I need to take my own advice and not focus on the surprise Christmas guest who will be arriving soon and instead concentrate on everyone around me. Scanning the room, I find the presents all opened and the kids disappearing in small groups to start playing with their new games and toys. Angelina hangs out near Storm and Landon, flipping through things on her phone, seemingly disinterested in the fanfare we still go through for the younger ones.

"It looks like everyone is done." I incline my head toward the kitchen. "The girls are going to start cooking now."

The incredible brunch spread we already enjoyed before opening gifts filled our stomachs well, but now, it's time to get ready for the massive Christmas feast Nana always prepares for Christmas dinner—which is my cue to stay far away from the kitchen.

Dani slides off Savage's lap and approaches us, her

eyebrows raised. "Nora, you going to go help Antonia, Skye, and Storm in the kitchen?"

Nora laughs and shakes her head. "Wasn't planning on it. Since they always ban you, I figured you, me, and Care would clean up all the wrapping paper in here and get the table ready."

Her sister scowls at her. "I was *not* banned from the kitchen."

Storm sticks her head around the corner and points a finger at her. "Yes, you were! We learned our lesson many, many years ago not to let you touch *anything.* Not even the salad!"

Dani glares in her direction but doesn't respond, just takes a sip of her mimosa. "Whatever. I can set a table."

Nora slips from my arms to join her, with Caroline following close behind, leaving me leaning against the mantle with my tonic and lime, staring at the twinkling white lights on the tree.

Gabe approaches, beer in hand, and rests his shoulder against the mantle next to me, examining the disaster the kids have left in their wake. "You would think now that they're all a bit older, they wouldn't make such a mess."

I chuckle and take a sip of my drink. "You're insane if you really thought that would ever happen. They're like Tasmanian devils, whirling in and whirling out of rooms, leaving destruction for the adults to clean up."

Angelina glances up at us and scowls. "Hey, I resent that blatant generalization!"

I point at her. "Present company excluded."

She pushes up from her chair and wanders out toward the sliding doors that lead to the back door, apparently not wanting to get stuck cleaning up after her little sister and cousins.

I don't blame her.

Gabe lifts the amber bottle to his lips, takes a drink, then sighs. "You seem distracted today."

To say the least.

And I thought I was doing a good job of covering it and was warning Nora not to let the kids see her rattled.

"I am." My gaze cuts to the closed front door. "This situation with the boy Luca and Byron found…"

Gabe nods slowly. "I haven't been able to stop thinking about it, either." He casts a quick glance around the room and steps closer. "But everyone should be able to rest a lot easier, knowing Luca took care of the father."

It takes a moment for his words to fully register.

Luca *took care of* the father…

All the air rushes from my lungs in a giant whoosh, and I dart my gaze to Nora, where she chatters with Dani and Caroline in the dining room, clearing off the table from brunch and resetting it for dinner.

Last night, Luca said he was going to track down Jude's father, but this is the first confirmation he succeeded in his righteous and violent endeavor.

I step closer to Gabe. "Already?"

He nods slowly and takes a giant drink from his beer, even though it's barely noon. "The dad came back to the club early this morning, looking for Jude..."

Shit.

It wasn't that I hadn't expected this, or that it wasn't warranted. If anyone deserves to end up full of bullets and dumped in the bayou, it's that piece of trash who called himself Jude's father.

But I hadn't anticipated it happening so fast.

One thing we've all learned over the years is that rash moves usually result in consequences we may not want to face. We're careful. Meticulous. We don't rush into anything—except apparently taking out abusive douchebags like Jude's dad.

"Does everyone else know?"

Gabe shakes his head. "Not yet. Luca let Savage and me know, but we didn't want to bring murder into our Christmas celebration right away this morning."

"Holy shit." I down the rest of my drink, wishing it were a glass of bourbon or even vodka at this point, after a decade and half of sobriety. "I'm glad the kid is safe. I just hope Luca did it right and I won't have to represent him in felony court."

A smirk tilts Gabe's lips. "You really think Luca would do anything stupid like leave evidence or get caught?"

Good point.

I shake my head. "No…"

Rubbing at the back of my neck, I look at Savage, where he talks with Saint and Landon. He nods at me, his jaw tight. I return a bob of my head, and we don't even have to speak for him to know that I'm now in the loop, which is likely what he's telling the other guys.

It may be Christmas and not the ideal time to be discussing Luca's late-night vengeance, but everyone's tense. Knowing that's been taken care of will certainly bring a much-needed sense of peace to the gathering.

A moment of silence lingers between us while Gabe watches the girls in the dining room across the foyer from us.

"You think Luca and Byron will have any trouble keeping Jude with them?"

I glance at him. "They shouldn't. I spoke with Judge Cramer in children's court personally last night, and I made a call to HSD this morning with his order."

Gabe raises a blond brow. "So, they're going to

give a kid to the former head of the mob and his husband...just like that?"

Scowling, I shake my head. "No, not *just like that*. It's a temporary order. They'll have to get approved as foster parents and go through all the proper certifications. If this ends up being a permanent thing, then... we'll see what happens."

Gabe snorts. "Luca with a kid." He takes a swig of his beer. "Now, Byron...*that* I can see. But Luca?"

I laugh and motion toward the open archway to the kitchen, where Skye busily bustles around with Storm and Mom, making dinner. "Did you really think *you* would be a father when you got together with Skye? I seem to remember you saying something about *never* having kids."

His lips droop into a frown. "No. I never thought I wanted that or that I'd be any good at it. But"—he shrugs—"things changed."

"Not enough for you to *marry* my sister, though. Just knock her up with twins..."

He rolls his eyes at me. "Ha, ha. Very funny. As we've said a hundred times, we aren't the marrying type, but you know your sister has me locked down for life."

I snort. "She better. You and Luca aren't the only ones who can make someone disappear."

Gabe's green eyes widen. "Wow, threats on Christmas Day. Now the party has really started!" He smacks me on the shoulder and grins. "I guess it wouldn't be a Hawke holiday without some."

Chuckling, I push off the mantle and point a finger at him. "Why don't you have another beer while I go find my *wife?*"

He smirks. "Going to drag her back to your old room for a nooner?"

I scowl at him. "You want me to tell Skye you said that?"

Gabe barks out a laugh. "You'd rat me out?" He shakes his head and motions toward the kitchen. "Actually, go ahead and tell her, and do it in front of Nana. I'm sure your mother would *love* to know what you two are always up to when you disappear back there to 'find something' or whatever excuses you make."

Waving him off, I wander into the dining room and slide up behind Nora, where she leans over the table, adjusting the runner down the middle of it. I brush my lips to her ear, inhaling her scent that always seems to calm me, even when I'm at my worst.

Murder may not be on the menu for most families on Christmas, but for *this* one, in *this* circumstance, it's the icing on the fruit cake.

"Luca took care of Jude's father."

She stiffens for a moment, then sags back against me, a weight lifting off her shoulders that I'm confident she wasn't even aware she's been carrying since Luca called us last night. "You're sure?"

I nod against her and press my lips to her cheek. "Gabe just told me. He's *safe*, angel. And now that he's with Luca and Byron, he always will be."

The Hawkes protect their own—blood or not.

At any cost.

CHAPTER 3

GABE

*S*kye bends over the open oven, messing with something in a pan inside of it, her beautiful ass swaying slightly in the air. It is way too tempting not to take advantage of her precarious position.

I sneak into the kitchen and smack one cheek hard enough to make her yelp and almost tumble forward into the oven. If I hadn't wrapped my arm around her waist and held her steady, she might have been face-first in the pan of baked clams.

She scowls back at me. "You dick."

Storm's laugh from the other side of the counter fills the space, quickly followed by Antonia tsking.

The matriarch of the Hawke family shakes her head, fighting a smile despite her reproachful look. "Will you two cut it out?"

I press a kiss to the back of Skye's neck as she rights herself, then walk over and wrap my arm around Antonia, squeezing her against me. "You want one, too, Nana?"

She elbows me playfully in the ribs. "I'm too old for you."

I kiss her on the cheek. "You? Never."

The woman who brought me into this family, who always accepted me as one of her own, from day one, rolls her eyes. "What are you doing in here, anyway?"

"I just came to harass Skye." I lift my empty bottle. "And to get another beer."

Skye closes the oven with her hip and tosses a pair of tongs onto the counter, then leans back against it, crossing her arms over her chest. That same look she's always given me—even back when she was a child and I was just Savage's best friend—overtakes her face. Her lips twist into a frown.

I raise my brows innocently. "What did I do?"

She taps her toe. "You know what you did?"

"What?"

One of her hands flies out toward the oven. "You almost knocked me into the damn stove."

I walk over and press her back against the counter,

dropping a kiss to her lips. "*Almost* being the key word here. I saved you."

She barks out a laugh and shoves at my chest. "Saved me. Yeah. Yeah. Right."

"Your life would be so boring without me, woman."

One of her dark brows rises in challenge. "Maybe I like boring."

Storm laughs from where she works on a pan of baked ziti. "Since when?"

Skye's eyes cut over to her sister then back to me. "Since the twins turned thirteen. They've been hellions, especially Atlas. I swear to God, that kid goes looking for fights. I could use some boring."

Nana glances over her shoulder, where she's working on assembling the lasagna. "I told you two, you never should have brought him to that boxing gym."

Oh, no. Here we go again.

"Ma"—I turn back to her—"he has a talent for it. We all saw it at a young age with him. I know you don't like boxing…"

She stiffens slightly, then returns her attention to the task at hand. "Boxing took Sam from me."

A moment of heavy silence hangs in the kitchen, and Storm walks over to her and wraps an arm around her mother's shoulders. "A freak accident in the ring took Dad from you. It's not going to happen again."

Antonia shakes her head. "You can't promise me that Atlas won't get hurt if he sticks with this."

Skye walks over and joins them, rubbing her mom's back. "No, we can't. But as we all know, there are other dangerous things in this world besides the boxing ring. We can't protect them from everything."

No one needs to specify what she's talking about.

I lean back against the counter and watch the Hawke women huddled together. Even after all these years, I can still feel the palpable pain of losing Star in the accident that almost took Savage from us, too. And even though Storm has found happiness again with Landon, the loss of Ben continues to tear at her and always will.

The agony we all suffered and the changes that happened to the entire family because of those events will reverberate through all of us forever.

It makes guilt at her worry over Atlas claw at my chest. As a father, I always worry about my kids, but I also know my son well enough to understand he won't stop, even if we try to make him. He's a born fighter, who definitely inherited that from the grandfather he never even met. Ignoring his natural ability would be trying to suppress a part of him. The ring calls to him in a way we can't brush aside.

I rub at my nape, trying to release some of the

tension suddenly there. "I'm making sure he's careful, Ma. Savage and I are working with him, sometimes Stone, and you know he has a great coach."

The same man who once coached his grandfather...

Antonia glances over her shoulder at me but doesn't say anything. She just returns to her work as the girls move away from her.

No one wants to ruin a holiday with this dark, heavy talk, which is why we've kept the full truth of what happened to Jude from the matriarch of the Hawke family. If she knew the depths of the depravity he's had to suffer during the mere ten years of his life, she wouldn't be able to keep it off her face when she meets him.

My phone buzzes in my pocket, and I glance at it —a text from Savage, who's just in the other room and could have come in here and spoken with me easily, which means it's something he doesn't want to say out loud.

SAVAGE

Luca and Byron are on their way with Jude. They got everything squared away with HSD.

I push off the counter and grab a beer from the refrigerator, then pop off the cap and take a long, cool pull from it. Skye watches me carefully, and I incline my head to indicate that she should follow me out of the kitchen.

Her eyes widen slightly, and she glances at her mom and Storm before she wipes her hands on a towel and follows me into the dining room, where Caroline, Nora, and Dani work on resetting the table.

I drag her into the corner and wrap my arms around her the best I can with the beer bottle in my hand.

"What?" She looks up at me.

"You're not really mad, are you?"

She shoves at my chest playfully. "Of course not. What's going on?"

"Luca and Byron are on their way with Jude…" For a split second, I consider not telling her about what Luca did until later, but everyone's been twisted up about this poor kid. She'll want to know what happened as soon as possible. "And the father is no longer a problem."

Her eyes widen slightly. "Okay, good. I mean, that's good."

I nod. "It is."

"Do you think we should warn the kids?"

I shake my head. "No. If we make a big deal about Jude coming today, they might overwhelm Jude with questions he can't answer. I think it's better if we make it *not* a big thing. Just allow them to show up and say he's staying with Luca and Byron for now.

Try to get the kids to play with him without turning it into a circus." I shrug. "I don't really know."

She nods slowly. "I think it's probably a good idea. You're right."

Grinning at her, I press a kiss on her forehead and squeeze her to me. "My two favorite words."

Skye playfully pinches my ribs. "Ha-fucking-ha!"

Storm sticks her head into the dining room, her dark brows raised. "Skye, you coming back to help?"

Dani raises a hand. "I can help."

Everyone turns toward her. "No," the chorus goes up, and Dani's jaw drops.

She props her hands on her hips looking incredulous. "Come on. There has to be something I can help with besides setting the goddamn table."

Storm shakes her head. "Stick with what you're good at."

Dani scowls, but everybody laughs it off like we do every holiday when she tries to make her way back into the kitchen, where she absolutely does not belong.

Nora walks over and bumps her sister's hip with her own. "Don't look so put out. You're very good at a lot of things. Cooking just isn't one of them."

Landon approaches Storm and whispers something in her ear that has her jerking back with wide eyes—likely the same thing I revealed to Skye.

Skye starts to pull out of my arms to follow her

sister back into the kitchen, but I tug her up against me and lower my mouth to her ear. "When we get home, you're going to bake some of my favorite cookies, right? Seeing you bent over that oven got me thinking about our first time together."

My cock grows between us, and she giggles and rubs against it. "Atlas and Astrid will be home tonight…"

I pull back and scowl. "Maybe we can arrange another sleepover for them at someone else's house."

Skye laughs and pushes away from me, leaving me to adjust my semi so it isn't obvious. I wander back out into the living room and over to where Savage talks with Saint, Landon, and Stone.

I stop next to my best friend. "So, they're on their way?"

Savage nods.

"Everyone knows now?"

Landon's blond head bobs. "I told Storm."

Saint nods. "I told Caroline."

Stone inclines his head toward the dining room. "I told Nora."

I look between all of them. "And we are all in agreement that we don't say anything to the kids?"

Savage rubs a hand across his stubbled jaw. "That's right."

Angelina pops her head into our little huddle, her

blue gaze darting to Savage. "What aren't you telling us?"

Shit.

I gently try to nudge her back. "Don't worry about it."

She scowls slightly. "You know, I'm twenty-two. I'm not a kid anymore."

Landon wraps his arm around his stepdaughter and tugs her up against him, pressing a kiss the top of her head. "You'll always be a kid, even when you're forty."

She looks up at him and gives him a saccharine sweet smile. "As if you'll be alive that long to see it, old man."

He feigns offense, pressing his hand over his chest. "Ouch. That one hurt."

She playfully elbows him, then walks away, probably to find something to entertain herself with that isn't one of the board games meant for her younger sister and cousins.

Angie is right; she isn't a kid anymore. She won't even let anyone call her "Angel" like we used to when she was a child. She's a young adult, and she probably should be brought in on what's happening, but I don't want to ruin her Christmas with the reality of what Jude suffered.

I stare out the window at all the lights in the yard and the fake Santa and reindeer on the lawn. Despite the warmth of the house and laughter and Christmas music filling it, a chill rolls down my spine and the hair on the back of my neck stands on end.

It's one of my feelings again, and I hate it.

It usually means something bad is coming, but this should be a joyous day, not one full of trepidation and worry.

I just need to shake it off and get in the spirit.

SKYE

Mom gives me a look as I return to the kitchen. "What's everyone whispering about?"

Shit.

I wince and cut my gaze to Storm, who gives me a look that tells me she knows, too, and plans to keep her mouth shut. "Nothing, Mom. Just that Byron and Luca will be here soon with Jude."

Not a complete lie.

That's *usually* the key to getting one by Antonia Hawke—keep a little bit of the truth in there.

Mom nods, eyeing me suspiciously, as I pull out the seasoned ricotta to start making the stuffed shells. Storm comes over to help, giving me another look that screams, *I hope she doesn't push this.*

Our mother is far too perceptive for her own good

sometimes. It's useless to try to keep things from her —same with Savage. Definitely an inherited trait.

Mom moves to the oven and slides in the lasagna, then turns back to me, crossing her arms over the "Kiss the Chef" apron Savage gave her for her birthday last year. "That's what Gabe had to pull you out of the kitchen to tell you?"

Too damn observant.

After raising five kids—six, if you count Gabe— she can see through pretty much all of us, and *everyone* has been off today.

Storm forces a smile and glances back at her. "It's nothing, Mom. Really. We're just excited to get everyone here to have dinner."

Again, not a lie.

We're all waiting for Byron and Luca on pins and needles.

I keep stuffing, avoiding looking at Mom so she won't be able to see my clear redirection of the conversation. "I grabbed a few things I had bought for the boys and wrapped them for Jude"—I cast a quick peek over my shoulder at Mom—"so he'd have something to open when he got here."

Mom's hard gaze softens. "That was very thoughtful of you. I'm sure he'll appreciate it. You say he doesn't have any family, right?"

I bite my lip to keep from vomiting the truth.

Storm nods. "That's my understanding, and it

appears he's going to stay with Luca and Byron, at least for a while."

It's another truth, just not all of it, and I can tell Mom wants to dig and ask more, but she doesn't, probably to avoid an argument on Christmas Day. There will be plenty of them, but she tries not to be the instigator.

She'll keep trying to pry it out of us, though, and eventually, someone will cave. It's inevitable where "Nana" is concerned.

She scans the kitchen as if it isn't the place she's most at home. "What else do we have left to do?"

I motion toward the stuffed shells. "Once these are done and in the oven, it should just be the salads, the garlic bread, and the pies."

Storm grabs the spoon from my hand. "I'll finish these. Why don't you go check on the kids and make sure they're not killing each other?"

Thank God.

Big sister saving me with an excuse to get out of here for a bit before I say something I shouldn't.

Mom leans to glance into the living room. "Can't the guys do that?"

I freeze.

Storm snorts. "They're busy doing whatever it is they do in the living room—mostly drink and grunt, I think."

Wiping off my hands on a kitchen towel, I wave

off Mom. "It's all right. I'll check on them and be right back."

Mom gives me another look, but she doesn't object as I slip out of the kitchen and make my way toward the sliding glass door that leads out onto the patio in the backyard, near the pool, where the kids tend to gather.

Kennedy, Bishop, Atlas, Astrid, Angelina, and Coen sit around the table, playing what appears to be poker. I point a finger at all of them. "You better hope Nana doesn't find you guys betting back here, especially with him sitting at the table." I point at Coen. "Why don't you go find Pope, Isaac, and Allie?"

Coen scowls and crosses his arms over his chest. Twelve going on thirty. He always wants to be with the older kids, even when we try to push him toward Pope and Allie. "I want to play."

Somehow, allowing them to teach him to gamble doesn't sound like something Stone and Nora would appreciate, not to mention Mom. "Well, I don't think that's a good idea."

He huffs again. "Then, I'm going to watch."

Angie walks over and leans toward me so no one else can hear. "I'll keep an eye on him. If things get too out of control, I'll send him in."

Even though Bishop and the twins aren't that much older than Coen, their maturity level means I have far less concern for them than him. Knowing

Ang will be monitoring the situation makes it a little easier to walk away. "Good. Thank you."

She raises a brow at me. "You want to tell me what's been going on? All the hush-hush whispering?"

I narrow my eyes on her. "Not particularly."

Angie scowls. "When are you guys going to stop treating me like a child?"

"Nobody treats you like a child."

She rolls her eyes. "Bullshit."

Coen's eyes widen.

I give her a chastising look. "Watch your mouth around him."

"Oh, yeah…" Angelina laughs. "Like any of you do."

"True." We all have a bad habit of speaking without filters around the kids, especially the older ones. "But still, we rely on you to take care of all the little ones, right?"

Her lips twist. "Yes."

"Would we do that if we thought of you as one of them? I know it's hard being the oldest and a full six years older than even Kennedy, but we appreciate you keeping an eye on them so we can handle other things, things you don't need to worry about."

Like the trauma the boy who will soon be joining the festivities has suffered.

She accepts the answer reluctantly, then grabs a chair next to Coen and whispers something to him that has him nodding. "Coen and I are going to play as a team. Okay?"

Atlas looks like he's about to argue, but I cut a glare at him that silences him on the spot. It's better to just let Coen play than to deal with him being crabby the rest of the day.

"All right, anybody need anything? Some snacks?"

A chorus of "yes" goes up, and I hustle back into the kitchen. "The kids are hungry. We have another, what, two hours before dinner's ready?"

Mom glances at the timer on the oven. "I'd say about that."

"I'm going to throw some chips into a bowl and toss it out there. Apparently Isaac, Pope, and Allie are off together somewhere. No fists flying, as far as I can tell."

But around here, that can quickly change.

This many people under one roof means there is always some sort of disagreement. Typically, they're good-natured and easily assuaged, but everyone, once in a while, someone has to step in to mediate. I'd love to avoid that today with all the other stressors floating around.

I find a bag of chips, empty it into a bowl, and bring it out to the kids.

At least for the moment, everyone seems content and happy, the kind of relaxed Christmas Day we can enjoy. Instead of heading back into the kitchen, I make my way down the hallway and pop my head into a couple of bedrooms until I find Isaac, Pope, and Allie in Savage's old room, sprawled out on the bed. "What are you guys doing?"

Isaac glances up at me, then Pope and Allie follow suit. "Just playing some of the games we all got."

Allie holds up a deck of cards. "I want to do *Uno*, but they want to play *Trouble*."

"Well, I think you guys have plenty of time to play everything before we eat." I narrow my eyes on the boys. "Right, boys?"

I focus *most* of my glare on Isaac. At his age, he should be able to prevent any arguments and be diplomatic about keeping the peace between the younger ones.

"Well, if you guys are hungry, I just put some chips outside with everyone else."

Isaac waves me off. "We're good."

They turn back to their game, ignoring me, and I pull the door halfway shut and make my way out to the living room, where the guys all cluster near the tree. The music pipes through the speakers, light and cheerful, not exactly matching the mood it's supposed to help create.

Gabe stares out the window, his shoulders tense.

I slip up behind him and wrap my arms around his waist, pressing my face against his shoulder blades. "Don't look so worried."

He glances back at me. "I'm trying not to."

"Really, everything's going to be fine."

We're all nervous about what will happen with the new arrival, who will be walking through the door soon, but worrying about it won't do anyone *any* good. Gabe has always gotten too far in his own head, and even after years of therapy, there are still times when he falls down dark holes that I desperately try to pull him out of.

"I know, but it's my responsibility to make sure everyone stays safe, and right now, things just feel"—he shrugs slightly—"a little off."

I squeeze him tightly. "I know how you get when you have one of these *feelings*, but you have to let it go, or you're going to ruin Christmas."

He grins at me. "I'm not going to ruin Christmas."

"Promise?"

He turns in my arms and takes my face in his palms, tilting it up to him. "I'll tell you what, I won't ruin Christmas as long as you figure out a way to get the kids to someone else's house tonight. Then you can bake for me like we talked about earlier"—he leans in and feathers his lips across mine—"preferably in the nude."

I smack his arm. "That sounds like burns in painful places just waiting to happen."

"I'll keep you safe, Skye." He grips my chin. "I always do."

The laugh bubbles from my lips before I can stop it. "Always?" I raise a brow. "I seem to remember rescuing *you* and saving *your* life when you were bleeding and almost dead in that godforsaken cabin in the bayou..."

He scowls at me. "And you will never let me live that down for the rest of my life, will you?"

I smile. "Of course, I won't. What fun would that be?"

CHAPTER 4

CAROLINE

I scan the dining room, my eyes bouncing over the bright-red and green table runner, the intricately folded napkins with hand-stitched Christmas trees on them, the delicate wine glasses, and the shining silverware all set in perfect place. A smile pulls at my lips, and I let my gaze drift over to Nora and Dani, where they place the last of the water glasses. "I think we did a decent job."

Dani nods, examining our handiwork, but then she looks toward the kitchen and scowls. "I could have helped in the kitchen."

I bark out a laugh and roll my eyes. "Will you get over it already? Let's go see what the boys are up to."

Nora laughs. "Probably no good. As always."

The laughter helps release a little bit of the tension we've all been feeling today. Holidays are always hectic around Nana's house, but this year, everything seems to be ratcheted up ten-fold.

No one knows what to expect when Luca and Byron show up, and all of us seem a bit on-edge waiting for them to arrive.

The girls follow me into the living room where Savage, Gabe, Stone, Landon, and Saint congregate near the tree, talking in low tones under the Christmas music piped over them.

Saint turns toward me as I approach and wraps a big arm around me, engulfing me against his massive frame. "They'll be here any minute."

I tense inadvertently, then try to relax in his familiar hold. "Good. I think dinner's going to be ready soon, too."

His stomach rumbles, and he presses a hand over it. "Good. I'm starving."

I laugh and pinch his ribs. "You're always hungry."

He flashes me a grin, then dips his head low so he can whisper in my ear. "I'm definitely still hungry for more of what I ate last night, too."

Heats floods my core as the memory of the way he spread me out on the kitchen counter and had *me* for dinner—and dessert—fill my head. Pressing my thighs together against the throb suddenly there, I shove at his chest. "Don't say things like that to me in this house. Nana hears *everything*."

He chuckles low, his whole body shaking. "The way you were screaming, she might've heard you from across town."

I toss him an annoyed look, but I can't fight the smile that pulls at my lips.

It's so rare we have a night without Pope and Bishop in the house. Having her sleeping over at Storm and Landon's and him at Gabe and Skye's gave us a nice little reprieve.

I didn't have to bite my tongue—or something else —to keep from alerting them to what their father does to me in the bedroom…or the kitchen.

"You have a filthy mind, Saint Clarke. You know that?"

He grins at me and lowers his head to press a kiss to my lips. "I do know that, Caroline Clarke."

But I wouldn't have it any other way—my brutally handsome yet gentle and generous husband has always been my protector and the only one who can completely destroy me in the best way possible.

Movement in the large picture window at the front of the room catches my attention, and I glance toward it and stiffen as Luca's car pulls to the curb.

"They're here."

All the conversation dies as everyone turns to look that way.

Saint scans the room. "We can't all stand here, staring at them. You're going to make the kid uncomfortable."

Savage nods. "You're right." He forces a smile. "Let's not make it a big deal."

Everyone tries to return to their conversation, but the slight tension still lingers in the room as we wait for the front door to open. I peek around Saint and watch the little boy, who can't be more than ten, climb from the back of the car slowly. Sandy-blond hair falls over his forehead, and he brushes it back to stare wide-eyed at the house.

Luca and Byron walk him to the path that leads up to Nana's house, and the boy freezes, staring at it like it's something he's never seen before. Even from here, I can see him shaking, and my stomach tightens.

That poor kid.

Everything he's been through...

I try not to think too much about it. If I do, I won't be able to fight back the tears.

Saint squeezes me, then tugs me against his chest, so I can't keep looking out the window. "Stop staring, Caroline."

I bury my face against him and release a heavy sigh. "I'm sorry. Let's talk about something to keep my mind off it."

He chuckles, making his chest vibrate against me. His warm, strong arms hold me steady, the same way they have for so many years, and immediately comfort me, releasing some of the anxiety. "Well, I was thinking…"

I look up at him. "Yeah?"

His dark eyes twinkle with mischief. "Maybe we make doing sleepovers at various houses more of a regular thing."

The promise in his gaze makes that heat flood my cheeks and between my legs again. "I think that's a good idea, but we'll have to *host* all the kids at some point."

And it's hard enough to find alone time with *two* in the house, let alone if we had the whole crew running around. Bishop can occupy herself practicing her jiu jitsu or tae kwon do, and Pope is constantly studying, but they always manage to need us at the most inopportune times. When all the kids are over, it's an absolute madhouse.

Saint offers a shrug of his wide shoulders. "I have ways to keep you quiet." He starts chuckling and brushes the hair back from my face. "You should have seen how wide your eyes just got, Bambi." He leans down and nips at my ear. "You going to run?"

I grin against his cheek at the memory of the familiar words and loop my arms around his neck. "No, I told you I'm never running again."

"I don't know, Bambi. But…I kind of like it when you make it hard for me."

"Oh, I have absolutely no trouble getting you hard."

His bark of laughter floats through the room, mingling with the sounds of "Rudolph the Red-Nosed Reindeer." The front door opens. I tense slightly, but Saint gives me a squeeze and glances over to the table in the corner where Gabe and Landon have settled to play a game of Scrabble.

"Maybe we should join them, so you don't stare at the kid."

I press my lips together. "Stop it. I'm good."

"Okay."

He watches me like he isn't so sure, and I peek around him as Luca, Byron, and Jude enter the foyer. Luca squats in front of the kid and says something to him I can't hear with the music filling my ears, then motions toward the dining room. Jude leans around the corner to examine it, and Luca pushes to his feet and leads him toward the kitchen.

The boy stares at us in the living room with wide, striking blue eyes, and Nora offers him a kind smile, though I can see the pain she's trying to hide after what she saw and knowing what she does about his history.

Nana will take care of him, though, and welcome him with open arms, just like she did with the rest of us—Saint, Luca, Byron, and me, even Gabe—none of us are Hawkes by blood, but we're Hawkes in every way that matters.

We are a part of this family that always has room for one more lost soul.

SAINT

Despite the holiday music floating around us, the barks of laughter, and the overall good vibes, tension still permeates the air. This family loves too hard and cares too much not to all feel deeply for Jude and what he's been through. Each and every one of us would take his pain on ourselves so he wouldn't have to suffer with it, but right now, all we can do is give him space and try to make him feel welcome without smothering him.

Byron enters the room, his gaze following Luca and Jude, and he releases a heavy sigh when he reaches us.

I raise a brow. "Everything okay?"

He rubs a hand on the back of his neck and shakes his head, his gaze cutting over to ensure Jude can't hear him. "I don't know. That's such a hard question."

Caroline slips through my arms and reaches out to give him a hug. "It'll work out. It always does, right?"

Byron shrugs. "I hope so. He's just so shut down…"

The true anguish in Byron's words claws at my chest.

For over a decade, I've protected this family, done everything in my power to ensure none of us ever gets hurt or put in the position we were in when Dom Abello was in control. I never want to see that kind of pain in anyone's eyes again, but here it is in Byron's.

I clap him on the shoulder. "It's only been a day. Give him some time."

Byron gives me a tight smile and nods.

"You and Luca are doing the right thing, the best thing for him."

Byron tenses slightly. "You guys know how I feel about Luca"—he swallows thickly—"doing anything that might drag him back into that life. But in this case"—a muscle in his jaw tics—"it's more than warranted."

He probably went too easy on that fucker...

It's on the tip of my tongue to ask exactly how Luca "took care" of Jude's father, but I'm sure I'll get all the dirty details later. Right now, all that matters is that the kid is safe here with us as well as in Luca and Byron's home—even if I would have ensured the man suffered a lot longer than the time Luca had with him.

Nana appears in the entryway to the kitchen with Jude at her side. He peeks toward the living room, his gaze darting to the floor almost immediately before he follows her down the back hallway.

"Where's Nana taking him?"

Caroline glances that way. "I think Pope, Isaac, and Allie are in one of the bedrooms playing. She must be going to introduce him."

Byron releases a heavy sigh of relief. "If anyone can get through to the boy, it'll be Allie, right?"

I grin at him. "That child is pure sunshine. So, yeah."

Luca comes out of the kitchen, staring down the hallway after Nana and Jude before he makes his way over to us.

I raise a brow. "How did he do meeting Nana?"

Knowing how welcoming that woman has always been to all of us, I can't imagine she wasn't the same with him.

A sigh slips from Luca's lips, and he gives a shrug that tells me he has no idea. "About as well as could be expected, I guess. He went with her. So..."

Byron reaches out and wraps his hand around Luca's arm, squeezing it. "Do you want to leave? Go back home? Is this too much for him?"

Luca shakes his head. "I think we give it a little bit of time, see if we can stay to eat. If he looks like he can't handle it, we'll go."

Caroline motions to a stack of presents under the tree. "Skye brought a few gifts for him, if you think he'd want to open them."

Byron and Luca share a look that makes unease tighten in my stomach.

"What is it?"

Luca rubs a hand across his jaw. "We got him a bunch of new clothes. Shoes. He had literally nothing. But he seemed uncomfortable with it. So, I don't know how he'd feel about gifts."

I nod. "I get it." I let my gaze wander over everyone gathered in the room, soaking up the warmth Antonia Hawke's house and the people in it always hold. "It was hard for me to accept when you all opened your arms to me."

Byron and Luca share a knowing look.

It seems like such a basic concept to be welcomed by a family, to be brought into the fold. But for some of us, it was never that simple.

Byron showed up here in New Orleans without anything or anyone and found a home at the Hawkeye Club. Luca's father forced him out of New Orleans when he was only Jude's age and basically disowned him to force Luca to build his life on his own. Caroline found a job and best friends here with Danika, and when I came to the U.S. at sixteen, searching for better opportunities than what Jamaica had for me, I never imagined I would now control over one hundred security personnel who work for the dozens of Hawke Enterprises businesses.

I'm the one keeping all these people safe, ensuring

our businesses are never threatened. They've put this trust in me, and I need to ensure they know it transfers over to the newest addition as well.

"You guys know if you need anything for him, security-wise, to let me know"—I quickly scan to ensure Nana and all the kids are out of the room, then look to Luca—"or if you need any help cleaning up."

Luca's dark eyes lock with mine. "I took care of it. It won't be a problem. But I appreciate the offer. As for security, I told Jude last night that he could lock his door to the guest bedroom."

"Did he?"

The corners of his lips twitch. "Immediately. I think it made him feel safer, and I'm all for that. I don't know if putting in additional security or having people around more would just scare him, though. He's already terrified of his father."

Caroline clings to me, her hands tightening on my arm. "He told you that?"

Byron shakes his head. "Not in so many words. But it's clear what was happening."

I rub Caroline's back, wishing I could have been there when Luca ended that piece of shit. The thought of anyone ever laying a hand on Bishop or Pope is enough to make me want to go kill the man all over again. "You're not going to tell him his father's gone, are you?"

Luca tenses. "No. I don't want him to be afraid of

us, too. All he knows right now is that HSD has approved him to stay with us for a while. The rest, we'll figure out later. I told him I talked to his father about him staying with us and that he doesn't need to worry about him. That's all he needs to know."

The Hawkes aren't above eliminating someone who really needs it—like Jude's father—but telling a ten-year-old you offed the man in order to protect him would only scare him more. He has no idea the lengths Luca and Byron will go to for him now that he's in their fold, the lengths any of us will go to.

Nana reappears from the hallway and pauses at the entrance to the living room, giving us all a smile. "He's back with Allie, Pope, and Isaac."

Luca raises a brow at her. "He okay?"

She gives a tight smile. "He will be…eventually. I'm confident of that."

And somehow, those words coming from Antonia Hawke are like a soothing balm settling over everyone in the room. All eyes turn away from her as we return to our previous conversations.

I tug Caroline against me again and bury my face in her hair. I've never felt luckier to have her or to be part of this family, to be a piece of something, a group that holds so much unconditional love for each other.

And on a day like today, it's impossible not to feel it radiating through the room along with the Christmas music.

CHAPTER 5

STORM

I blink away the tears I managed to hold in until Mom left the kitchen with Jude as I work on mixing the salad, and she returns and walks over to me to wrap her arm around my shoulders.

"Hide those tears, Storm. You don't need him seeing them."

Shit.

I nod sharply and drop the spoon to swipe them away, then turn toward her. "I'm sorry, Mom. I just... his eyes."

So full of fear and empty of anything else...

I know what that's like, to feel empty, lost, alone. After Ben died, nothing, not even Angelina, could pull me from the black abyss I found myself in. For so long, I lingered there, hoping to join him, but then Landon came along and changed everything. He allowed me to live again and see how much joy I had all around me with these people, especially Angie.

Mom squeezes me and gives me a soft smile. "You all are keeping whatever happened to that boy from me. I don't know why you thought I wouldn't see it."

Maybe because none of us really knew how bad it would be except Stone and Nora.

I release a heavy sigh. "We didn't want to upset you on Christmas, Mom."

She presses her lips into a thin line. Even in her seventies, the woman can still freeze you with a single look. "After everything I've been through in this life— losing your father and Star, almost losing Savage. Gabe almost dying. Then losing Ben..."

At the mention of his name, my chest tightens, but unlike in the beginning, when hearing it would bring nothing but pain, now I'm able to smile and remember the good times and incredible gift he gave me by loving me and leaving me with Angelina.

Mom swallows thickly, fighting her own emotions. "Do you really think I couldn't handle knowing the truth about what happened to Jude?"

The tears for what that little boy has suffered return, and I swipe them away again in case he reappears in the kitchen. "It isn't that, Mom. We just..."

Try to protect her the way she always protected us.

Skye approaches and thankfully interjects before I'm forced to try to explain it to her. She wraps her arm around Mom's shoulders and squeezes. "We didn't want to ruin the holiday." She smiles. "Everyone's trying to keep the mood up."

Mom's eyes dart between us, and she finally releases a sigh. "Before this day is over, *someone* is going to fill me in."

Or she'll overhear enough to figure it out herself.

Skye kisses Mom on the cheek. "Okay, Ma. I'll make sure you get filled in later. You brought Jude back to Allie, Pope, and Isaac?"

She nods. "Yes, and of course, Allie practically launched herself at him."

I can't fight my laughter, and warmth now replaces that sense of dread that has been sitting on my chest. "If anyone can make him feel at home with us, it'll be her."

Mom squeezes my shoulder. "That was my thought, too. You have a wonderful daughter."

Skye's jaw drops. "Oh, what, and Astrid is chopped liver?"

Mom scowls as she walks over to the oven and pulls it open to check on the lasagna. She slams it closed. "No. Astrid is probably the most genuinely kind-hearted person I've ever met, but she's a teenager, and she and Atlas have developed a bit of an attitude as of late."

I chuckle and point at my younger sister. "She's got you there. Allie's still young enough to be sweet and innocent."

Angelina appears at the entry to the kitchen and scans the counters. "Mom, you ready for my help?"

"Yes." I motion toward the lettuce and other salad ingredients spread out across the cutting board to my right. "I need you to make the salad and start bringing some things to the table. Can you grab your sister and have her come help, too?"

Angie gives me a once-over, narrowing her eyes on me—probably easily seeing the signs of my recent tears. But she thankfully gives me a reprieve from the third degree. "Got it." She leans out to peek in the living room. "Where is she?"

I force a smile that I hope Ang buys. "One of the bedrooms, with the boys."

"All right." Casting another questioning look at us, she disappears down the hallway to find Alessandra.

Everything's almost ready, and dinner can't come soon enough. All the tension in the house waiting for Luca and Byron to arrive with Jude needs to break, and the laughter and good-natured ribbing that always happens around the Hawke family table is a great way to do that.

I scan the kitchen. "Anything else we need, Mom?"

She frowns. "It sounds like we're going to need a few extra bottles of wine."

My bark of laughter makes her jump slightly. "That's probably true. I'll go grab some from the wine fridge."

And check on the "boys," who have been left unattended for far too long in the living room.

I make my way out of the kitchen and find Saint, Caroline, and Savage talking with Luca and Byron while Gabe and Landon bicker over a game of *Scrabble* at the corner table.

Fighting a grin, I sneak up behind Landon and scan his letters, then lean in and whisper in his ear, "Ecstasy, triple word score."

He jerks his head up toward me, his eyes wide. "Wow. How did I miss that?"

The corners of my lips curl up, remembering the shower last night, and I slide my arms around his neck and down his chest to whisper in his ear again. "I don't know. You never seem to have any problem giving it to me." I lean down and press a kiss to his grin. "You guys doing okay?"

He nods and glances back toward the hallway. "Yeah, I saw Ang go back there. What was she doing? Looking for Allie?"

Before I can answer, Angie reappears, her brow furrowed, and walks into the room, bee-lining toward us, but Savage turns away from his conversation with Luca and Byron and raises a hand, stopping her.

"You need something, Ang?"

Her lips twist, and she scans the room. "Has anyone seen Allie?"

My chest immediately tightens. While Allie has always been a bit reckless and precocious, she usually doesn't disappear. She sticks to Pope like glue when she isn't with Angie.

Savage shakes his head, looking my way. "No. Why?"

Angie shrugs. "Isaac and Pope said she went after Jude."

Luca and Byron exchange a look that sends a shiver through me as Savage drums his finger on his knees.

Byron climbs from his seat. "We'll help you find him."

He steps up to Luca and whispers something in his ear, and Luca nods and gives him a tight smile, his already dark eyes darkening more than usual.

They approach Angie, and Savage motions toward the bedrooms. "Angelina and I will check the house." His gaze darts to Luca and Byron. "You two check outside and ask the other kids out there if anyone has seen them."

Everyone nods their agreement, and Byron and Luca beeline for the front and back doors while

Savage follows Angie down the hall toward the bedrooms.

I start to pull away. "I should go after them, help them look for Allie."

Landon reaches out and grabs my arm. "No." He shakes his head. "Too many people he doesn't know descending on them. Leave him be."

Worry eats a pit in my stomach, but I release a heavy sigh as Landon's grip tightens around my arm. "If he's with Allie, he's fine, and I'm sure they'll find them. They can't have gone far."

"I know. I just…"

Landon's soft-green eyes—the ones that dragged me out of the abyss—meet mine, and he tugs me down onto his lap, wrapping his arm around me. Gabe watches us from across the table but doesn't say anything as Landon feathers his lips against my ear.

"You, of all people, should know that this family can bring anyone back from what they think is unlivable, right?"

His words claw at that old scar, the one from losing Ben that can never be erased, and he tightens his grip on me. "The boy will be okay. I promise. Hawkes always rise, right?"

I nod. "Hawkes always rise."

He presses a kiss to my lips, and I slide off his lap. He smacks my ass. "Now, get back to the kitchen where you belong."

I laugh and roll my eyes at him.

That man can always break the tension.

He brought me back from the brink of losing myself, and now, hopefully our daughters will do the same for Jude.

LANDON

Angelina carefully scoops out a little bit of each dish from the table onto two plates while the rest of us slowly pick at our food. Everything is just as delicious as always, but the empty chair where Alessandra usually sits and the one next to hers that Nana put out for Jude are giant elephants in the room.

Storm's gaze remains locked on her eldest daughter. I know she wants to jump in and offer to help her making the plates for Allie and Jude, but Angie has already made it very clear that she thinks no one else should go back to interrupt them.

I'm not entirely sure how I feel about them eating in a dark closet, but if that's what it takes to make Jude comfortable, then that's what is going to happen.

Ang finishes by adding a piece of garlic bread to each plate, then lifts them from the table.

I push my chair back and hold a hand out to stop Storm from doing the same. She's too emotional about Jude to go back there. "I'll grab a couple of sodas, so they have something to drink."

It will save a trip, and I want to check on Allie —even if I keep telling Storm she's fine and not to.

Angie hesitates for a moment. "That's a great idea. Thanks, Landon."

That little pang that always hits me square in the chest when she doesn't call me "Dad" after all these years returns, but I brush it aside, the same way I always do.

Because I understand why.

I may have stepped in and taken over that role after she lost her father, but I'll never replace him and would never even try. Ben became a Hawke the moment Storm saw him and fell in love with him, and Angelina is the best of both of them.

She may not be my flesh and blood, but she's mine in every way that matters, even if she can never think of me as "Dad."

I move to the kitchen and grab a couple of Cokes, then head down the short hallway to the bedroom that used to belong to Storm. Angie's soft voice floats out the cracked door, and I slip in to find her on her knees in front of the open closet door, talking quietly with Allie and Jude.

For a moment, I lean against the jamb and watch her, pride swelling in my heart for the strong, thoughtful woman she's become. She hands the plates to them, and I clear my throat.

She glances over her shoulder at me. "My stepdad brought you guys some sodas."

I make my way over and squat next to her. Jude and Allie sit with their backs against the closet wall, plates on their laps. Jude gives me a dubious look, but Allie grins.

"This is my dad."

Jude looks over at her and back at me, but he doesn't say anything.

"Hey, buddy." I set the drinks on the floor in front of each of them and give him a little half-wave. "I'm Landon. I'm glad you could join us today."

Allie rests her plate on her legs and grabs her soda. "Thanks, Dad."

I reach in and ruffle her hair. "You're welcome, kiddo. You two enjoy."

Angie smiles. "I'll bring you pie later."

She and I both push up to our feet, and Angie slides the doors halfway closed again, sealing the kids back inside but allowing a sliver of light to stay on them. She follows me out into the hallway and pulls the bedroom door shut behind her. We make it a few steps down the hall before she releases a heavy sigh and leans back against the wall, closing her eyes.

I stop in my tracks and take a step back toward her. "Are you all right?"

Her lids flutter open, and she looks up at me with tears shimmering in her eyes. "I don't know."

"I saw you talking with Luca earlier."

She pulls her bottom lip between her teeth and nods. "Yeah. He said…" She trails off. "He said Jude's dad did something to him."

I grind my jaw to keep the truth from slipping out. Angie may be an adult now. She may be capable of handling and processing what really happened to Jude, but it isn't really for any of us to be telling it to the kids.

It isn't fair to him to have everyone know.

Only the adults do because we need to protect him, to ensure that nothing like this can ever happen to him again, so that we make sure we're careful with him and give him everything he needs.

"I think Jude will be fine. He seems to really enjoy your sister."

Angie grins. "Yeah. I have a feeling if he sticks around for a while, they'll be thick as thieves."

I wrap my arm around her shoulders and urge her down the hallway back toward the dining room, where the clank of silverware against plates echoes out to us. "I know this has been an unusual Christmas with everything going on, but I want you to know how much your mom and I appreciate what you're doing for him and for Allie."

"I'm not doing anything."

I pull her to a stop before we hit the dining room. "Yes, you are. Whatever happened to Jude…he needed somewhere safe. And he found it. You're helping protect that space for him—even if it is in a closet. That means a lot."

Tears well in her eyes, and she swipes them away. "You gave me that, too."

A vice tightens around my heart. "What do you mean?"

Her lips tremble. "I know it's hard for me to show it sometimes because"—she swallows a sob—"I really miss my dad, especially on days like this when I can still remember sitting on his lap and opening presents. But I'll never forget what you did for my mom and for me. Before you came along, she was broken. And I don't think she would've put herself back together if it hadn't been for you."

They're the words I've always wanted to hear, that I've spent almost fifteen years hoping were true.

And now, my eyes burn with tears that match hers. I reach out and pull her to me, squeezing her tightly and pressing a kiss to the top of her head. "I love you, kiddo, you and Allie and your mom, more than anything."

She nods. "I know."

"And you never have to apologize to me for how you feel about your dad. Okay?"

She nods and squeezes me back, then releases me

as we both try to wipe away the evidence of our little heart-to-heart.

"Let's go eat. Okay?"

Her head bobs in agreement, and we slip back into the dining room. I had hoped we'd do so without drawing any attention, but all eyes turn our way.

Nana raises a brow from the head of the table. "Everything okay back there?"

I smile. "Yep."

Angie nods. "Yep. They're eating. I told them I'd bring them pie."

Nana smiles. "Good. It wouldn't be Christmas without a piece of my apple pie, right?"

Everybody murmurs their agreement, and my gaze immediately darts to Storm, who watches me carefully, her eyes bouncing between Angie and me. She knows something else happened. The woman can read me and her daughter way too well to let it slip past her.

The moment I retake my seat, Storm slides her hand over my thigh and squeezes it, leaning in. "Are you two okay?"

I drop a kiss on her cheek. "Better than okay. I promise. And Allie's fine."

"Good."

Savage clears his throat from where he sits at the foot of the table, across from his mother. His bright-blue eyes scan over every one of us, and he raises his wine glass. "I'd like to make a toast."

Everyone drops their silverware and grabs their glasses, even the kids, whose glasses are filled with sparkling grape juice.

"I know this Christmas has offered us a surprise, but I just wanted to say how happy I am that everyone has stepped up and done their part to welcome Jude for as long as he may be with us."

His gaze darts to Luca and Byron, who exchange a look.

I can see it in their eyes—they already care about him far too much to ever let him go, just like I did the first moment I met Storm and Angie. From the moment I saw Storm at that party, I knew she was my future, despite her complicated past and how broken she was, how reluctant she was to let me in.

Grief doesn't follow a linear timeline, and Jude's recovery from what's happened to him won't be, either, but if anyone can help, it's the people around this table.

Savage inclines his cup toward us. "To the Hawkes. Merry Christmas, everyone."

"To the Hawkes," the chorus goes up, and everyone takes a sip.

CHAPTER 6

BYRON

*T*he laughter and raucous arguments floating from the game of *Pictionary* in the living room follow me down the hallway to Storm's old bedroom. I pause outside the closed door.

Maybe I should just leave them alone.

I glance at my watch.

But they've been in there for three hours, without either of them coming out, so I should at least check on them.

I slowly turn the knob with a shaking hand and push it open, pausing to listen for a moment.

Allie's light, lyrical voice floats through the cracked closet doors. "And then Angie told me I wasn't allowed to use her makeup anymore, but she got a whole new kit this morning. So, I'm going to ask Mom if I can have her old stuff. I think that's fair, don't you?"

I grin as I wait for Jude's response, but he either offers none or it's said so softly that I can't hear it.

One thing Allie will always do is chatter someone's ear off, but it seems not to have bothered Jude the last few hours.

I start to pull the door closed, and it releases a squeak that makes me freeze and wince. Allie stops talking, and the closet door opens.

She pops her dark head out, her bright-blue eyes landing on me. "Oh, hi, Uncle Byron."

"You guys okay in here?" I scan the empty pie plates sitting just outside the door.

At least he's eating.

Allie bites her lip and glances back toward where Jude must be. "I need to go to the bathroom."

I chuckle and step in. "Go."

She hesitates for a second, then pushes the door the rest of the way open and climbs to her feet. Her eyes dart to Jude. "I'll be right back."

Sweet kid.

Even at ten, she can tell Jude needs the reassurance and is sure to give it to him. It's intuitive for her. No one needed to tell her what to do for him; she just *did* it.

Allie moves past me out into the hallway as I slowly approach the open closet. I squat until I can see Jude tucked in the corner behind the hanging clothes, knees pulled up to his chest, staring at me. "You okay, buddy?"

He stares at me for a second, then nods.

I offer him a soft smile. "Good. You get enough to eat?"

He nods again.

"Nana's a great cook, isn't she?"

He swallows thickly and nods. "She is."

Those two words are more than he's spoken to us since we first found him. After explaining what he was doing there, he's been practically catatonic. It appears Allie's constant chatter has relieved a bit of the tension he felt when we got here—though, his current position suggests it's going to take a hell of a lot more to actually get him to feel comfortable.

I rest my arms on my knees and offer him a smile. "I know you don't really know Luca and me, or any of the Hawkes, but I want you to understand that you're safe here and welcome." I point absently toward the living room. "We even have some gifts for you under the tree, if you want to open them."

He tenses, fear returning to his blue gaze.

"I could bring them in here so you wouldn't have to go out where everyone else is."

His shoulders relax slightly, but he still shakes his head.

"Would you like me to bring them back to our place for later?"

He nods, and despite the tears threatening to well in my eyes, I force another smile. "That sounds like a good plan. We'll be leaving soon, okay?"

He bobs his head again.

"Are you having fun with Allie?"

Maybe *fun* isn't the right word, but apparently, I really suck at this talking-to-kids thing, despite having practice with all nine of my nieces and nephews.

The last twenty-four hours, I feel like I've been stumbling over, and over, and over again. I'm sure Luca and I have said and done the wrong things a thousand times. I try not to think about what he ultimately did to Jude's father as I stare at the traumatized boy who has filled my heart with so much I never thought I'd experience.

He considers my question for a second, then nods again.

"Good."

Allie comes up behind me. "What's good?"

I push to my feet and let her slip past me, back into the closet. "Jude said he's having a good time with you."

Her face lights up, and she grins. "Me, too."

She settles next to him and reaches out to take his hand in hers, interlocking their fingers and squeezing it tightly. His fingers whiten as he squeezes back.

Thank God.

For a split second, I can see the possibility that he'll really make it through this okay.

But *not* if he gets dumped into some foster home. Not if he gets bounced around until he ages out of the system and never has a solid, safe place to land. The really *great* foster families are few and far between around here, and I don't have any faith that anyone will put the time and effort in with him that it will take to save him from the dark hole he's locked himself into in his head.

This little boy needs us.

He needs the *Hawkes.*

I pull the door almost closed, leaving it open a tiny crack. "We're going to leave in a little bit, Al, okay?"

"Okay, Uncle Byron."

Her constant chatter fills the closet again, and I slip from the room, not bothering to fight my grin.

"Sleigh!"

"Reindeer!"

"Light bulb!"

Everyone's shouting voices float out from the living room, and I rejoin them to find the game of *Pictionary* still in full swing—though, I can't tell for the fucking life of me what Gabe drew on the board. And apparently, no one else can, either.

But there's no sign of Luca or Savage.

I check the empty dining room and the kitchen, where Antonia, Storm, and Skye work on cleaning dishes. "Have you guys seen Luca or Savage?"

Antonia glances up. "I think they're out back."

Probably sharing a drink away from the fray, which doesn't sound like a bad idea.

I pause at the bar set up in the dining room and pour myself an Ardbeg, hoping the smoky scotch will help ease away some of the worry filling me. More yelling comes from the living room, and I take a sip and make my way outside to find Luca seated on one of the lounge chairs near the pool, Savage next to him.

The chilly late-December air sends a shiver down my spine as I slowly lower myself onto the chair on the other side of Luca.

He glances at me with a furrowed brow. "Where were you?"

"Checking on Jude and Allie."

His shoulders instantly tense, and the dark eyes I know almost as well as my own narrow on me. "Are they okay?"

I nod. "They seem to be, but I think we should get out of here before too long. It's been a lot for him."

Luca's jaw tenses, and his hand tightens around

his tumbler, likely full of the same thing I'm drinking. Something crosses his gaze that makes my stomach tighten—a look I haven't seen in years. One I hoped to never see again.

Savage doesn't miss it, either. "You did the right thing."

Even though Luca and I both hear his words, I don't know if either of us believe them.

Luca looks up at him. "I'm not so sure."

Savage scowls. "The man abused his son. The man made him do things that no human should *ever* make another do. There was only one way that was ever going to end where any of us would be content with it."

A heavy sigh slips from Luca's mouth, filled with a thousand feelings I know must be welling inside him right now, and he takes a long sip from his drink.

He gave up the violence of the mob for me, for us, so that we could have a life together without constantly looking over our shoulders. So that I wouldn't end up dead on the street with another bullet hole in me. But we've also paid the price for his past.

The constant whispers.

The dirty looks.

People who still won't work with the Hawkes because he's involved with them.

And now, we've got this boy to think about—the

boy who now has no one *because* of us. That guilt weighs on him as heavily as it does me, even if we both know, deep down, that it was the right thing to do.

I just hope he doesn't allow it to eat him alive the way I did when I hid my relationship with him from the people I care about the most.

LUCA

A few stars twinkle in the dark sky through the cloud cover, and I stare up at them and release a heavy breath, trying to let some of the stress and uncertainty of the last twenty-four hours go with it.

I haven't even attempted to sleep since I laid eyes on Jude yesterday, and I wouldn't have been able to even if I hadn't been busy with...other things.

All I see when I close my eyes is him.

The way he cowered behind that dumpster, terrified of me finding him and discovering what he was doing,.

How his body shook when I grabbed his arm and brought him into the club and to my office.

His terrified gaze following every move Byron or I made, like he was anticipating having to run.

I've seen fear in a lot of people's eyes over my lifetime, people who knew what was coming and suffered far worse fates at my hands, but there was something about the way Jude looked at me, petrified but also begging for help, that wouldn't let me look away.

And now, here we are, and I have no fucking idea what to do about it.

I glance over at Byron, who offers me a tight smile. This has been rough on him, too, even though he wasn't the one who had to get his hands bloody. He carries the weight of knowing what I did, of what we agreed to do, as soon as we found out what happened to Jude.

Byron reaches out and rests his hand on my arm. "I think…" He swallows thickly and glances at Savage and back at me. "I think we need to keep him."

It's the same thing I've been thinking, but neither of us has had the guts to say it. We both felt it the moment we met him, and somehow, we knew, deep in the pit of our stomachs, that this was somehow meant to happen.

I nod. "I think so, too. But I don't even know… shit!" I shake my head and scrub my hand across my face. "How would we even go about doing this legally? What court is going to grant Luca Abello custody of a ten-year-old kid? Hell, *any* kid?"

It's why Byron and I have never even considered the possibility of having a family. We always assumed it was out of our reach because of my past, that we would have to pay that penance for the life I chose.

But this is different.

Savage nods slowly. "We'll talk to Stone. We know enough people, Judge Cramer, our friends at HSD. We can figure something out to make it happen."

I push off from the lounge chair and start pacing beside the pool while Savage and Byron watch me. Even another sip of the strong scotch doesn't help quell my frustration.

The sliding glass door opens, and Stone steps out, his eyes darting across all of us as he comes to join and stands beside his brother. "What's going on out here?"

Savage gives him a half-grin. "I'm pretty sure Luca and Byron just decided they want to adopt Jude."

Stone's eyes widen slightly, and his gaze cuts between us.

I rub my hand at the back of my neck as I pace back and forth, back and forth, my Italian loafers scraping along the concrete pool decking. "Do you think it's possible?"

He crosses his arms over his chest and nods. "Yeah. I mean, HSD already approved you for temporary emergency custody. You'll have to jump through all the hoops, but since the father won't be a problem anymore..." He trails off slightly. "I think we can make it happen if that's what Jude wants."

I freeze mid-step and whirl to face Byron. "Shit. What if he doesn't?"

Byron's shoulders slump slightly, and he rests his elbows on his knees, steepling his fingers in front of his face. "I hadn't even thought of that. He was so scared of us last night, petrified of the whole situation. He barely even spoke two words to Nora other than when she told him she needed to know to make sure he was okay. He wouldn't even speak to us unless absolutely necessary. He's spent the whole day in the damn closet with Allie. Maybe this isn't what's best for him. Maybe he should—"

"No." Savage's interjection carries through the night air. "He's a Hawke now. This is what's best for him, and you both know it. We *all* do. We can take care of him, all of us. Together."

His insistence relieves some of the tension in my chest.

I've seen what the Hawkes can do, how they bring people under their wings and make them part of the family. I've experienced what it's like to seek their forgiveness and receive it. I've felt the love that radiates from everyone in this house, and Jude will, too. Eventually.

"You're right. From the moment I saw him, I just felt...God, this is going to make me sound like a fucking pussy." I shrug. "I felt complete. Like this is what has been missing."

I glance at Byron, hopeful he doesn't take that the wrong way and think that our relationship somehow hasn't been enough for me.

But he just smiles. "And here I thought I was the only one who felt that way."

"Definitely not."

And I should have known better than to ever doubt Byron would be one hundred percent on board with me on this.

We've created a fantastic life together, and with the Hawkes, we're building an empire that will last for generations. But we've never had anyone to leave any of it to. We've done it for ourselves, for everyone else's kids, thinking we could never have our own. And this feels...right.

Stone walks over and claps me on the back. "Then we'll start on the paperwork tomorrow."

"That easy?"

He offers a half shrug. "Nothing's ever easy about being a parent, which you two are about to fucking learn." He barks out a laugh and shakes his head. "You have no idea what's in store for you."

"Gee, thanks."

He squeezes my shoulder. "I'm just trying to prepare you, bud. Parenthood is"—he grins—"the greatest thing that's ever happened to me. Besides Nora, of course."

"Of course."

The glass door slides open, and Nora's blonde head pops out. "Oh, there you are. What are all you guys doing out here?" She steps out, rubbing her bare arms. "It's fucking freezing. Come inside. We've given up on *Pictionary*, and I think we're going to play *Clue*, try to track down the killer."

She says it with a playful glint in her eye, but I can't help the tension it brings to my chest. Byron stands and comes over to me, leaning in as Stone and Savage make their way back toward the house.

"You did the right thing. Don't ever think you didn't."

I let my eyes meet his, hoping he can't see how gripped by fear I really am right now. "What if you're wrong? What if Jude finds out and never forgives me? Never forgives us?"

"Then we'll have to live with that, knowing it was what was best for him."

"I hope you're right."

"I usually am." He grins at me. "That's why you married me, right?"

I smirk, remembering the night we met at that dive and I took him back to my hotel room. "Amongst other reasons."

"Will you two hurry up?" Nora scowls from the open door, motioning us in.

Byron brushes his lips across mine. "One quick game, then we get him out of here and back home."

Home.

Our home—where he can feel safe, for maybe the first time ever.

I follow Byron in and slide the door closed behind me, then join everyone in the living room, including Nana, Storm, Skye, and all the kids, who are already splitting off into teams since there are far too many of us to play otherwise.

The bickering and laughter mingle with the Christmas carols still piped through the speakers and fill the house with so much warmth, it almost brings tears to my eyes.

This is what the Hawkes are all about, and Savage was right—Jude *is* one now.

Forever.

We don't let people go.

And we never give up on them.

I HOPE you enjoyed the *Hawke Family Christmas* novella and the brief introduction to the second generation of the Hawkes.

The Hawke Family Second Generation Series is now LIVE! You can start it FREE right now with *Night Hawke*, available at all retailers. Get yours here to see what happens with the next gen: books2read. com/NightHawke

To stay up to date on news, sales, and releases from Gwyn, join her newsletter here: www.gwynmc namee.com/newsletter

ABOUT THE AUTHOR

Gwyn McNamee is an attorney, writer, wife, and mother (to one human baby and two fur babies). Originally from the Midwest, Gwyn relocated to her husband's home town of Las Vegas in 2015 and is enjoying her respite from the cold and snow. Gwyn loves to write stories with a bit of suspense and action mingled with romance and heat. When she isn't either writing or voraciously devouring any books she can get her hands on, Gwyn is busy adding to her tattoo collection, golfing, and stirring up trouble with her perfect mix of sweetness and sarcasm (usually while wearing heels).

Website: http://www.gwynmcnamee.com/

Facebook: https://www.facebook.com/AuthorGwynMcNamee/

FB Reader Group: https://www.facebook.com/groups/1667380963540655/

Tiktok: https://www.tiktok.com/@authorgwynmcnamee

Newsletter: www.gwynmcnamee.com/newsletter

Instagram: https://www.instagram.com/gwynmcnamee

Bookbub: https://www.bookbub.com/authors/gwynmcnamee

OTHER WORKS BY GWYN MCNAMEE

Billionaires of New Orleans:

The Hawke Family Series

Savage Collision **(The Hawke Family - Book One)**

He's everything she didn't know she wanted. She's everything he thought he could never have.

The last thing I expect when I walk into The Hawkeye Club is to fall head over heels in lust. It's supposed to be a rescue mission. I have to get my baby sister off the pole, into some clothes, and out of the grasp of the pussy peddler who somehow manipulated her into stripping. But the moment I see Savage Hawke and verbally spar with him, my ability to remain rational flies out the window and my libido takes center stage. I've never wanted a relationship—my time is better spent focusing on taking down the scum running this city—but what I want and what I need are apparently two different things.

Danika Eriksson storms into my office in her high heels and on her high horse. Her holier-than-thou attitude and accusations should offend me, but instead, I can't get her out of my head or my heart. Her incomparable drive, take-no prisoners attitude, and blatant honesty captivate me and hold me prisoner. I should steer clear, but my self-preservation instinct is apparently dead—which is exactly what our relationship will be once she knows everything. It's only a matter of time.

The truth doesn't always set you free. Sometimes, it just royally screws you.

AVAILABLE AT ALL RETAILERS:

books2read.com/SavageCollision

Tortured Skye (The Hawke Family - Book Two)

She's always been off-limits. He's always just out of reach.

Falling in love with Gabe Anderson was as easy as breathing. Fighting my feelings for my brother's best friend was agonizingly hard. I never imagined giving in to my desire for him would cause such a destructive ripple effect. That kiss was my grasp at a lifeline—something, anything to hold me steady in my crumbling life. Now, I have to suffer with the fallout while trying to convince him it's all worth the consequences.

Guilt overwhelms me—over what I've done, the lives I've taken, and more than anything, over my feelings for Skye Hawke. Craving my best friend's little sister is insanely self-destructive. It never should have happened, but since the moment she kissed me, I haven't been able to get her out of my mind. If I take what I want, I risk losing everything. If I don't, I'll lose her and a piece of myself. The raging storm threatening to rain down on the city is nothing compared to the one that will come from my decision.

Love can be torture, but sometimes, love is the only thing that can save you.

AVAILABLE AT ALL RETAILERS:

Books2read.com/Tortured-Skye

Stone Sober (The Hawke Family - Book Three)

She's innocent and sweet. He's dark and depraved.

Stone Hawke is precisely the kind of man women are warned about— handsome, intelligent, arrogant, and intricately entangled with some dangerous people. I should stay away, but he manages to strip my soul bare with just a look and dominates my thoughts. Bad decisions are in my past. My life is (mostly) on track, even if it is no longer the one to medical school. I can't allow myself to cave to the fierce pull and ardent attraction I feel toward the youngest Hawke.

Nora Eriksson is off-limits, and not just because she's my brother's employee and sister-in-law. Despite the fact she's stripping at The Hawkeye Club, she has an innocent and pure heart. Normally, the only thing that appeals to me about innocence is the opportunity to taint it. But not when it comes to Nora. I can't expose her to the filth permeating my life. There are too many things I can't control, things completely out of my hands. She doesn't deserve any of it, but the power she holds over me is stronger than any addiction.

The hardest battles we fight are often with ourselves, but only through defeating our own demons can we find true peace.

AVAILABLE AT ALL RETAILERS:

books2read.com/StoneSober

Building Storm (The Hawke Family - Book Four)

She hasn't been living. He's looking for a way to forget it all.

My life went up in flames. All I'm left with is my daughter and ashes. The simple act of breathing is so excruciating, there are days I wish I could stop altogether. So I have no business being at the party, and I definitely shouldn't be in the arms of the handsome stranger. When his lips meet mine, he breathes life into me for the first time since the day the inferno disintegrated my world. But loving again isn't in the cards, and there are even greater dangers to face than trying to keep Landon McCabe out of my heart.

Running is my only option. I have to get away from Chicago and the betrayal that shattered my world. I need a new life-one without attachments. The vibrancy of New Orleans convinces me it's possible to start over. Yet in all the excitement of a new city, it's Storm Hawke's dark, sad beauty that draws me in. She isn't looking for love, and we both need a hot, sweaty release without feelings getting involved. But even the best laid plans fail, and life can leave you burned.

Love can build, and love can destroy. But in the end, love is what raises you from the ashes.

AVAILABLE AT ALL RETAILERS:

books2read.com/BuildingStorm

Tainted Saint (The Hawke Family - Book Five)

He's searching for absolution. She wants her happily ever after.

Solomon Clarke goes by Saint, though he's anything but. After lusting for him from afar, the masquerade party affords me the anonymity to pursue that attraction without worrying about the fall-out of hooking-up with the bouncer from the Hawkeye Club. From the second he lays his eyes and hands on me, I'm helpless to resist him. Even burying myself in a dangerous investigation can't erase the memory of our combustible connection and one night together. The only problem… he has no idea who I am.

Caroline Brooks thinks I don't see her watching me, the way her eyes rake over me with appreciation. But I've noticed, and the party is the perfect opportunity to unleash the desire I've kept reined in for so damn long. It also sets off a series of events no one sees coming. Events that leave those I love hurting because of my failures. While the guilt eats away at my soul, Caroline continues to weigh on my heart. That woman may be the death of me, but oh, what a way to go.

Life isn't always clean, and sometimes, it takes a saint to do the dirty work.

AVAILABLE AT ALL RETAILERS:

books2read.com/TaintedSaint

Steele Resolve (The Hawke Family - Book Six)

For one man, power is king. For the other, loyalty reigns.

Mob boss Luca "Steele" Abello isn't just dangerous—he's lethal. A master manipulator, liar, and user, no one should trust a word that comes out of his mouth. Yet, I can't get him out of my head. The time we spent together before I knew his true identity is seared into my brain. His touch. His voice. They haunt my every waking hour and occupy my dreams. So does my guilt. I'm literally sleeping with the enemy and betraying the only family I've ever had. When I come clean, it will be the end of me.

Byron Harris is a distraction I can't afford. I never should have let it go beyond that first night, but I couldn't stay away. Even when I learned who he was, when the *only* option was to end things, I kept going back, risking his life and mine to continue our indiscretion. The truth of what I am could get us both killed, but being with the man who's such an integral part of the Hawke family is even more terrifying. The only people I've ever cared about are on opposing sides, and I'm the rift that could end their friendship forever.

Love is a battlefield isn't just a saying. For some, it's a reality.

AVAILABLE AT ALL RETAILERS:

books2read.com/SteeleResolve

You can find information on the rest of Gwyn's books on her website:

www.gwynmcnamee.com